Mountain Wedding

Faye Gibbons
illustrated by Ted Rand

Morrow Junior Books
New York

Watercolors were used for the full-color illustrations.
The text type is 14.5-point Figural Book.

Text copyright © 1996 by Faye Gibbons
Illustrations copyright © 1996 by Ted Rand

Printed in Hong Kong by South China Printing Company (1988) Ltd.

1 2 3 4 5 6 7 8 9 10

Library of Congress Cataloging-in-Publication Data
Gibbons, Faye.
Mountain wedding/Faye Gibbons; illustrated by Ted Rand.
p. cm.
Summary: The children from two mountain families about to be joined in a wedding
change their minds about each other only after all of them together cooperate in a rescue.
ISBN 0-688-11348-6 (trade)—ISBN 0-688-11349-4 (library)
[1. Weddings—Fiction.   2. Mountain life—Fiction.   3. Family life—Fiction.]
I. Rand, Ted, ill.   II. Title.   PZ7.G33913Mo 1996   [E]—dc20   95-18197   CIP AC

To Dr. Joan Nist and my sister Jean Gagliano,
who share my love of stories,
and to Mary Lisby, who put me on the trail of this one
—F.G.

For the Nelson family
—T.R.

It was spring in the mountains when Mama married Mr. Long. All over north Georgia dogwoods were bursting into bloom and mockingbirds were courting and mating and feuding over nesting places.

They weren't the only ones fussing. Me and my brothers and sisters were fighting the children of the widower who was trying to take our father's place.

At the preacher's house that day, we stood in two scowling lines— Mr. Long's seven, in their best overalls and hand-me-down dresses, and the five of us Searcys in our mended city clothes. Larry Ray, Hattie, Bonnie, me, and Robert eyed them across the preacher's yard.

They made faces. We
made faces back. I was the one
Mama caught. "Mandy," she
said.

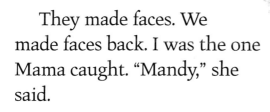

Mama was all decked out in her best dress and Sunday hat, with new ribbons to hide the frayed spots and a bunch of fresh flowers to cover a hole. Her eyes were smiling.

Mr. Long wore his brother's suit. It was too short and smelled like mothballs. And as he swatted at several honeybees circling Mama's hat, a seam ripped.

The preacher and his wife inspected us all and then looked at Mr. Long's wagon tied to a post of the well house. It was piled high with Long and Searcy belongings.

The preacher cleared his throat and opened his Bible. "We
are gathered together . . . ," he began in his church voice.

"Wait," said Mama, grabbing at my baby brother, Larry Ray, who had just
thrown himself on top of Mr. Long's next-to-the-youngest boy, Earl. The two of
them were tumbling over and over in the dirt and had rolled under the porch,
where they knocked into a big yellow tomcat. The cat hissed and a hound dog
on the porch growled in reply. A cluster of chickens in the yard clucked in alarm.

More honeybees arrived while Mama and Mr. Long dusted off Larry Ray and Earl and lined us all up again. Bees whizzed around the wagon, and Mr. Long's mules backed up in their traces until the narrow post they were tied to strained and trembled.

"Is everybody ready for the wedding?" the preacher asked.

"No!" answered all us children together. That's one thing we agreed on.

But Mama and Mr. Long both said yes, so the preacher hunted for his place in his Bible.

The yellow cat crawled from beneath the porch and padded his way across the yard with his tail erect.

"We are gathered together . . . ,"
the preacher began, just as a new
cloud of honeybees came flying
over the roof of the house and
onto the porch.

Suddenly the dog sprang to
life. *"Yip-yip-yip-yip-yip!"* he
howled, leaping from the porch
in a swarm of bees and racing
across the yard. The chickens
squawked and scattered, flapping
in every direction. Claws spread,
the rooster flew at the cat.

"*Ft-t-t-t!*" hissed the cat, making for the
wagon in a yellow streak.

He skidded on the wagon seat, sweeping off two hens before
clawing his way over a mattress to the top of a wardrobe.

All us children whooped with laughter.

Suddenly the mules lunged backward in the traces, the post snapped, and the well house crashed to the ground.

The mules raced around the yard, spilling a box,
a ladder-back chair, and two bags out of the wagon before
galloping off up the road, trailing a plume of dust.

Nobody was laughing now.

"Whoa!" bellowed Mr. Long, running after the wagon.

"My furniture!" cried Mama. She hitched up her skirt and lit out, too.

All us young'uns joined the chase, and the preacher huffed and puffed along behind. "Stop!" he yelled, waving his Bible in the air. "What about the wedding?"

Nobody answered and nobody stopped. We ran past woods and pastures and newly furrowed fields, gathering up a trail of Long and Searcy belongings as we went. Hattie scooped up our checkerboard and their dipper.

Robert picked up our bed sheet and their clock.

The Longs grabbed up our tablecloth and their
water bucket, our books and their lantern. I ran back
to get the youngest Long, Mary Lucy, who had stumbled
and skinned her knee. She put her dusty little hand in
mine, and we ran on together.

By the time we got to the creek, where the mules had finally stopped, we were all mixed and mingled into one big dirty group.

Mr. Long's young'uns looked at us Searcys and then at one another, and all of us began to laugh.

The preacher arrived as Mr. Long
tied the mules to a tree near the edge
of the creek. "Are we ready for the
wedding?" he panted.

"Yes," said all us children.
"Yes," said Mama. "We are finally gathered together."
And we were.